MAC ★ BARNETT

HOW THIS BOOK

ADAM ★ REX

MADE

Based on a True Story

WAS

SCHOLASTIC INC.

For Marina Addison  —M.B.

For Henry  —A.R.

SOME INFORMATION ABOUT HOW *HOW THIS BOOK WAS MADE* WAS MADE
In the interest of accuracy, we offer the following notes and corrections:
1. Although this book was originally printed in Malaysia, the edition you are holding
now was printed in the United States of America.
2. Adam Rex no longer owns the glasses he's shown wearing in this book. They broke on
a roller coaster.
3. The stuff about the tiger remains just as true now as ever.

ISBN 978-1-338-23262-2

Text copyright © 2016 by Mac Barnett. Illustrations copyright © 2016 by Adam Rex.
All rights reserved. Published by Scholastic Inc., 557 Broadway, New York, NY 10012,
by arrangement with Hyperion Books for Children, an imprint of Disney Book Group.
SCHOLASTIC and associated logos are trademarks and/or registered trademarks of
Scholastic Inc.

The publisher does not have any control over and does not assume any responsibility
for author or third-party websites or their content.

12 11 10 9 8 7 6 5 4 3 2                                    18 19 20 21 22

Printed in the U.S.A.                                              40

First Scholastic printing, November 2017

The art in this book was mostly made with black Prismacolor pencil on colored paper,
acrylic paint on a globe, photography, and Photoshop.

Hand lettering by Adam Rex

Ideas can come at funny times.

When I had the idea for this book, I went to a quiet place and I wrote.

I wrote from early in the morning until late at night.

It was very hard work.

Soon I had a bunch of words on paper. Those words were a first draft.

The first draft of this book was not so good.

Neither was the second draft.
Or the third.
Or the twelfth.

But writing lots of drafts is a useful part of the writing process. For instance, when the tiger came back for revenge because I beat him in arm wrestling, I burned these drafts and scared him away.

I worked and I worked, and with the twenty-first draft I was done. So I sent my words to my editor in New York City.
An editor tells you what parts of your story are good and what parts you need to fix.

She is like a teacher, only she works in a skyscraper and is always eating fancy lunches.

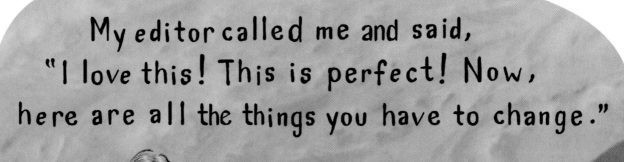

My editor called me and said, "I love this! This is perfect! Now, here are all the things you have to change."

And she sent the story back to me.

I took some of her advice.

And I ignored some of her advice.

And then I sent the story back to her.

And I said I didn't think they were good ideas.

And she said I thought they were great ideas.

And I said well let's agree to disagree.

And she said let's agree with me.

And I said
you're not the boss of me.

And it went back and forth
and back and forth and
back and forth...

until most of the
United States of America
was crossed out.

Eventually my editor loved all my words.

And I loved all my words.

Even
the tiger, who
had returned with
a posse, loved all my
words.

I was finished writing!
But this book was still not a book.
The words needed pictures. So my editor in New York
sent them to an illustrator in Arizona.

I sat around and waited.

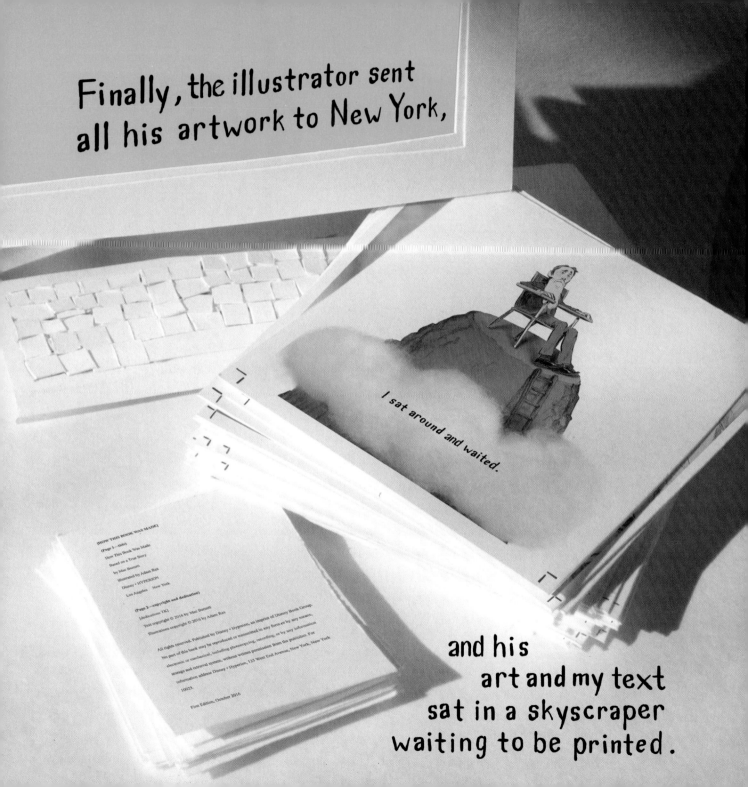

Finally, the illustrator sent all his artwork to New York,

I sat around and waited.

and his art and my text sat in a skyscraper waiting to be printed.

[HOW THIS BOOK WAS MADE]

(Page 1—title)

How This Book Was Made

Based on a True Story

by Mac Barnett

Illustrated by Adam Rex

Disney • HYPERION

Los Angeles   New York

(Page 2—copyright and dedication)

[dedications TK]

Text copyright © 2016 by Mac Barnett

Illustrations copyright © 2016 by Adam Rex

All rights reserved. Published by Disney • Hyperion, an imprint of Disney Book Group. No part of this book may be reproduced or transmitted in any form or by any means, electronic or mechanical, including photocopying, recording, or by any information storage and retrieval system, without written permission from the publisher. For information address Disney • Hyperion, 125 West End Avenue, New York, New York 10023.

First Edition, October 2016

Now: The fastest way to get this book to bookstores and libraries would be to print it nearby, in New York

or **Philadelphia**

or maybe even Miami.

But
this book was
printed
in

Malaysia

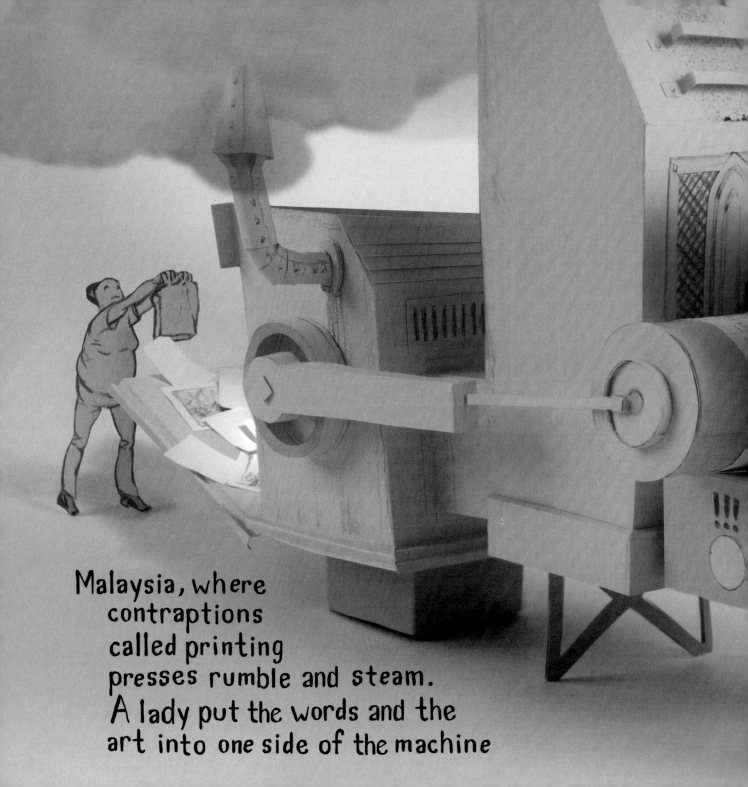

Malaysia, where contraptions called printing presses rumble and steam. A lady put the words and the art into one side of the machine

And then another book. And another. And another. Thousands and thousands of books. This book was buried below a great pile so tall you could see it from space. Astronauts looked down at Earth that day and saw a stack of books and the Great Wall of China, right next to each other. They smiled, then floated around a bunch while eating astronaut ice cream.

But that's science! This is literature.
And at last this book was ready to be read!
It needed to get to the United States as fast
as it could.  Of course,
the fastest way would be to put them on a jet.

But this book
got put on a boat.

A slow boat
took all the
books across the sea.

The journey
was dull.

Until the pirates arrived.

The pirates swarmed the boat and
quickly overran it. They tied up
the crew and stole the captain's keys.

The lead buccaneer kicked open the hatch to the ship's hold.

The pirates held their breath and imagined their treasure.

There was no gold inside, just books. Pirates don't read. So they sailed away.

An eagle swooped down and grabbed this book for her babies.

(To eat, not to read. Eagles don't read books either.)

She
ripped out a corner,
but her chicks didn't
like it. They pushed
this book out of
their nest.

to a truck driver whose load was one book short.

He made his delivery to a woman who put it on a shelf next to many other books.

This book waited.

And I waited.

And the tiger waited, and his posse waited, and the pirates and astronauts and the editor waited, and the illustrator and the old lady and her dog waited, and the truck driver and the angry ink-splattered Americans and the family of eagles and the people in Malaysia — they waited, we all waited, here in this book, which was practically bursting, just waiting for someone to open it. Because a book can have words and pictures and paper and tigers, but a book still isn't a book,

not really,

until it has a reader.

and you read this book
through to the very last page,

which was how this
book was made.

Mac Barnett

## HOW THIS AUTHOR WAS MADE

This author was made in California. His parents met in the Navy—his mom was a nurse and his dad was a doctor and they both took care of babies whose births had gone wrong. This author's birth went wrong. And so his parents worked together—his mother, exhausted and weakened by the ordeal, rising out of the delivery bed—to save this author's life. But this author wasn't an author yet. He was just a baby. After that it was books—many, many books—that made that kid an author.

Adam Rex

## HOW THIS ILLUSTRATOR WAS MADE

Well, his parents were on vacation at a lake. His brother was fast asleep in another room of the cabin, and it was a pretty night. He was born breech. He doesn't know if this is important, but his mother brings it up a lot. He was praised from an early age for his drawing ability, and practiced for 10,000 hours. He got a BFA in illustration from the University of Arizona, and practiced another 10,000 hours. Now he lives with his family in Tucson, which is not relevant to how he became an illustrator, necessarily—but it's a good last line for a bio.